THE BLACK APP

Hardive

JOSIO JOTI

BLUEROSE PUBLISHERS
India | U.K.

For permissions requests or inquiries regarding this publication, please contact:

BLUEROSE PUBLISHERS
www.BlueRoseONE.com
info@bluerosepublishers.com
+91 8882 898 898
+4407342408967

ISBN: 978-93-6452-999-0

Cover Design: Sadhna Kumari
Typesetting: Pooja Sharma

First Edition: October 2024

JOSIO JOTI INDUSTRY OF STORY AND SONG WRITING (JIS²W)

PRODUCTION

PRESENT A HALLOWEEN SPECIAL

THE BLACK APP

(HARDIVE)

DEDICATION

I would like to begin by expressing my heartfelt gratitude to God for His unwavering faithfulness in my life. His guidance has been a constant source of strength throughout my journey.

I extend my deepest appreciation to my parents, especially my mother, whose encouragement has inspired me to explore and develop my writing skills. This journey has not been without its challenges, but her belief in me has been a guiding light.

I am incredibly thankful for my friends in Nigeria, particularly the Set 2k24 group and my supporters from Deeper Life High School. Your enthusiasm for my stories and your willingness to read my work have motivated me to hone my writing talent. I am still on this path of improvement, and I am hopeful for what lies ahead.

To my friends in the UK—Leah, Latifat, Precious Abdullahi, Promise, Tinotenda, Amara, Oluwatimilehin, and Kemi—thank you for your relentless encouragement and for pushing me to pursue my dream of becoming a writer. Your support has been invaluable.

I would also like to give a special shout-out to Etuele Elozino Daphane, who helped design this impressive book cover. Your creativity and vision have truly enhanced this project.

Additionally, I want to acknowledge Osasenaga, Barnabas, Maxwell, Lois, and Ufuoma. Your constant encouragement to strive for improvement and to publish my work has been instrumental in my journey. I am deeply grateful for your support.

Finally, I want to thank each and every one of you for purchasing this book and for taking the time to review it. Your feedback means the world to me, and I sincerely hope you enjoy reading it as much as I enjoyed writing it.

Thank you all!

PREFACE

This books motivation was actually the writers excitement that comes when he imagines a scenario with if the person had a power, honestly I have never experienced racism but I made it all up how it would feel if someone was discriminated against and found a way to get what they deserve so that they don't receive the discrimination for long but unfortunately this decision lead to the daughter feeling guilt for something she didn't know how to control.

CONTENTS

CHAPTER ONE

"Many years ago, peace reigned in the lands until one young woman grew weary of the cruel treatment her husband endured due to his complexion," the narrator began, as the flash book flickered to life.

In a cozy apartment bathed in warm afternoon light, Miley sat curled up on the sofa, losing herself in the pages of a well-worn novel. The gentle rustle of turning pages and the soft ticking of the clock were the only sounds breaking the tranquil silence. Suddenly, a sharp knock at the door shattered her reverie.

"Who is it?" Miley called out, her voice tinged with curiosity. She carefully placed her book face-down on the coffee table, preserving her place, and padded towards the door. As she swung it open, her heart leapt into her throat.

There stood Kelly, her beloved husband, his normally cheerful face marred by angry bruises and a split lip. His shoulders sagged with exhaustion and defeat.

"Kelly, dear God, what happened to you?" Miley gasped, her voice trembling with a mixture of shock and concern. She gently ushered him inside, her hands fluttering anxiously over his injuries.

Kelly winced as he sank into a chair, his eyes downcast. "The police," he muttered, his voice thick with pain and frustration. "They beat me up at the store, accused me of being a criminal. It wasn't until the owner intervened that they finally backed off."

As Kelly recounted the harrowing incident,

The small kiosk shop buzzed with nervous energy as customers milled about, their eyes darting towards the entrance. Suddenly, two police officers burst through the door, their faces set in grim determination. Without hesitation, they zeroed in on Kelly, who stood frozen near the counter.

"Hey, you!" one officer barked, his finger jabbing accusingly in Kelly's direction. Confusion and fear flashed across Kelly's face as he pointed to himself, silently questioning if he was indeed the target of their attention.

"Of course, you," the other officer sneered, his voice dripping with contempt. "Don't play dumb with us, boy."

Before Kelly could utter a word in his defense, the officers lunged forward, their batons raised. The sickening thud of wood against flesh echoed through the shop as they struck Kelly repeatedly. He crumpled to the ground, arms raised in a futile attempt to protect himself from the onslaught.

To Kelly's horror, several customers began to cheer, their faces twisted with ugly satisfaction at the sight of his pain. Others who shared his complexion fled the scene in terror, pushing past one another in their desperation to escape a similar fate.

"Stop that! He is not the one. Stop it!" the storekeeper's voice suddenly cut through the chaos. The elderly man's face was flushed with righteous anger as he rushed towards the scene.

The officers paused, exchanging uncertain glances before backing away without a word of apology. As they retreated, the air hung heavy with tension and unspoken accusations.

The storekeeper, his hands trembling slightly, helped Kelly to his feet. Kelly's face was a mask of pain and humiliation, a trickle of blood running from his split lip.

But the ordeal wasn't over. As Kelly struggled to regain his balance, several customers began pelting him with bananas, their laughter cruel and mocking. The yellow fruit thudded against his battered body, a final indignity heaped upon the injustice he had just endured.

The vivid flashback faded, replaced by Miley's voice, thick with fury and anguish at the memory of her husband's suffering.

Miley's blood began to boil. The injustice of it all, the casual cruelty inflicted upon her husband simply because of his skin color, ignited a fierce rage within her.

"This has to stop," she declared, her voice quivering with barely contained anger. "My own parents refuse to visit us because I married a Black man. How much more hatred and discrimination must we endure?"

Kelly reached out, taking her trembling hands in his. "I understand your anger, my love," he said softly, his eyes filled with a mixture of pain and compassion. "But we must not let bitterness consume us. We must have faith that justice will prevail."

Miley pulled away, her frustration boiling over. "Faith? In what? A God who sits idly by while His children suffer?" she spat, her words laced with venom.

Kelly's face fell, a shadow of hurt crossing his features. "Please, don't speak that way," he pleaded. "Our faith is what gives us strength in these dark times."

As night fell, the couple lay in bed, the weight of the day's events hanging heavy between them. Miley turned to Kelly, her voice barely above a whisper. "I'm sorry for my outburst earlier," she murmured, tears glistening in her eyes. "I just can't bear to see you hurt like this."

Kelly pulled her close, his embrace warm and forgiving. "I understand, my love," he soothed. "But remember, hatred only breeds more hatred. We must be the change we wish to see in the world."

As Kelly drifted off to sleep, Miley's mind raced with conflicting emotions. Love for her husband warred with the burning desire for retribution against those who had wronged him. In the depths of her heart, a dangerous seed of vengeance began to take root

CHAPTER TWO

On October 31st, the atmosphere in the clinic was thick with anticipation and anxiety. Miley had been admitted days earlier, her body weary yet resilient, as she prepared to bring new life into the world. The sterile scent of antiseptic hung in the air, mingling with the faint sound of distant cries from newborns.

Kelly arrived at the hospital, his heart racing, and entered Miley's room, where he found her resting peacefully, a serene expression gracing her face. He took a moment to admire her, his heart swelling with love and admiration for the woman who was about to become a mother.

A few minutes later, the door swung open, and the doctor entered, pushing a small cradle accompanied by a nurse.

"I've got good news for Mr. and Mrs. Storkina," the doctor announced, his voice brightening the room. "You have a bouncing baby girl." As the nurse gently placed the baby in Miley's arms, tears of joy filled her eyes.

"My love, I will call you Melaangel," Miley whispered, her voice tender and filled with hope.

"What does that mean?" Kelly asked, intrigued, knowing his wife had a gift for languages.

"It means 'my angel,'" she replied, a slight tremor in her voice as she concealed the truth behind her choice of name.

As the years passed, Melaangel grew into a beautiful young woman. But as she turned 16, a shadow fell over her life. She began to notice that her friends drifted away without explanation, and each boy she dated would suddenly shout, "Leave me alone!" before running off in fear. Heartbroken and confused, Melaangel felt the weight of isolation pressing down on her. In a moment of desperation, she ran away, leaving her parents devastated and searching for answers. Never to be heard from again.

Seven years later, Miley gave birth to a son, whom she named Abel. As she cradled him in her arms, tears streamed down her face. Kelly, taken aback by her sudden emotional outburst, asked, "Why are you crying? You have a son. Isn't that a reason to be joyful?"

"Easy for you to say," she mumbled, her voice thick with unspoken grief.

"If it's about Melaangel, I'm sorry we couldn't find her," Kelly said gently, hoping to comfort her.

"That's not the problem," Miley replied, her voice trembling. "I have something to tell you. Remember when I said people would suffer for how they treat us?"

"Yes," Kelly answered, his brow furrowing in concern.

"I met a witch who told me I would need someone for it to work," Miley confessed, her eyes wide with fear.

"And who was it?" Kelly asked, dread creeping into his heart as he began to piece the puzzle together. Realization dawned on him, and he gasped, "No way! So you cursed our daughter?"

"Yes, and I am so sorry. Please find her and help her. I know you are the only one who can save her," Miley pleaded, desperation lacing her words.

"That's not the problem. You need to repent," Kelly said firmly, holding her cold hands in his, feeling a chill run through him. She closed her eyes and spoke silently her lips slowly stopped moving then panic surged as he noticed her hands growing colder. "No, it cannot be. She is dead. Please wake up!" he cried, his voice cracking as Abel began to wail in his arms.

Nurses rushed in, their faces a blur of urgency as they took Miley away to the emergency room. A few agonizing minutes later, the doctor returned, his expression grave. "I'm so sorry. She didn't make it."

Kelly's heart shattered. "How will I live if Abel never saw his mother?" he lamented, cradling the newborn as if he could shield him from the harsh reality.

"But before she passed, she said Melaangel means 'angel of death' in Kurdish and that you should change it when you find her," the doctor added, his voice steady yet compassionate.

"That's a lie. She said it means 'my angel,'" Kelly replied, his voice rising in anguish as he stormed out, the weight of loss suffocating him.

At home, he paced the living room, his mind racing with grief and anger. Suddenly, a figure appeared, its presence chilling the air. "I know you are surprised, but do not worry. I only came to tell you what she said is true, and if you value your life, do not try to change her name, or else you're next," she warned, her laughter echoing in the empty room as she vanished.

Years later, on Abel's twelfth birthday, Kelly sat him down and shared the painful truth about his sister, revealing the darkness that lingered over their family. "You can help her," he urged, his voice thick with emotion. And so, the story continued, a haunting reminder of love, loss, and the desperate quest for redemption. The End. the housekeeper, Nancy, concluded as the flash book ended.

CHAPTER THREE

Many years later,

A young boy named Hadie found himself running through the halls of his school, down to the path that leads to the school back where the garden is located his heart pounding in his chest as he desperately tried to escape the relentless pursuit of his tormentor.

"Leave me alone!" Hadie pleaded, his voice cracking with fear and exhaustion.

"Then give me your lunch money," the bully demanded, his words dripping with malice.

Hadie's stomach twisted with anxiety as he replied, "I didn't get lunch money today." The desperation in his voice was palpable, a mixture of fear and shame at his bad behaviour that has led to this effect.

The bully's face contorted with anger and disbelief. "You have the nerve not to get lunch money?" he sneered, his eyes narrowing dangerously.

Suddenly, two more boys appeared in front of Hadie, their faces twisted with cruel anticipation. They grabbed him roughly, their fingers digging into his arms. "Let me go!" Hadie shouted, panic rising in his throat.

"Oh, so you think you can get away that easily?" the lead bully taunted, circling Hadie like a predator stalking its prey.

Desperation clawed at Hadie's insides as he tried to explain, "Please, let me go. My parents refused to give me lunch money as punishment." The words tasted bitter in his mouth, a reminder of the constant disappointment he seemed to be to his family.

"Derek the wimp has no lunch money. How pitiful," the bully mocked, his voice dripping with disdain. Without warning, fists began to rain down on Hadie, each blow a reminder of his powerlessness and isolation.

As Hadie lay on the ground, his body aching and his spirit broken, he felt as if his life was flashing before his eyes. Every moment of rejection, every harsh word from his parents, every lonely day at school – it all swirled together in a dizzying kaleidoscope of pain and regret.

Three agonizing hours passed before Hadie finally managed to pull himself to his feet. The streets were dark and empty, mirroring the hollowness he felt inside. Each step towards home was a struggle, his bruised body protesting with every movement.

Entering the house quietly, Hadie prayed he could slip unnoticed to the sanctuary of his room. But his mother's sharp eyes caught him from her perch on the sofa, where she sat bathed in the flickering light of the television. "How was school today?" she asked, her tone deceptively casual.

"It was pleasant," Hadie lied, the words tasting like ash in his mouth. He hated deceiving her, but the truth seemed too heavy, too complicated to explain.

His mother's eyes narrowed suspiciously. "Then why are you late?" she demanded, her voice rising with anger.

"I... I... I was with my friends," Hadie stammered, desperately grasping for an excuse that might placate her.

His mother's face hardened, her words cutting like knives. "Oh, so your friends can take care of you better than me? Then you better start living with them," she spat, oblivious to the pain etched across her son's face, the bruises hidden beneath his clothes.

Later that evening, Hadie's father returned from work, his presence filling the house with a tense energy. "Hadie, come down here," he called from the doorway, his voice brooking no argument.

Hadie emerged from his room, his body screaming in protest with each movement. "Yes, Dad?" he replied, trying to keep the tremor from his voice.

"Come with me. I need your help with something on the computer," his father said gruffly, leading the way to the small office where their ancient desktop sat.

As Hadie gingerly lowered himself into a chair, his father turned on the computer, the ancient machine whirring to life. "I want you to open my email for me," his father instructed, impatience already creeping into his tone.

"Which email?" Hadie asked hesitantly, knowing that any wrong move could trigger his father's volatile temper.

His father's face clouded with disappointment and frustration. "You're studying IT. You're supposed to know how to do it," he snapped, his words a stinging reminder of the impossible expectations placed upon Hadie's shoulders.

After several tense minutes of fumbling and muttered instructions, Hadie managed to help his father access his email. Without so much as a word of thanks, his father dismissed him, leaving Hadie to retreat once more to the solitude of his room.

Alone at last, Hadie paced the confines of his small bedroom, his mind a whirlwind of conflicting emotions and unanswerable questions. The weight of his existence pressed down upon him, threatening to crush his spirit entirely.

"Why am I like this?" he whispered to the empty room, his voice choked with unshed tears. "Is this how my life is supposed to be? Am I really their child, or am I just a slave to their expectations?"

The questions tumbled from his lips, each one more painful than the last. "Why do my parents expect so much from me when I can't deliver? How can I change that? Haven't I already tried to change my ways, and it still didn't work out?"

Hadie's gaze fell upon the small mirror hanging on his wall, and he barely recognized the battered, hollow-eyed boy staring back at him. The bruises from the day's beating were already darkening, a physical manifestation of the pain that seemed to permeate every aspect of his life.

As night fell and the house grew quiet, Hadie lay on his bed, staring at the ceiling. The loneliness and despair threatened to overwhelm him, but somewhere deep inside, a tiny spark of resilience refused to be extinguished. He knew that tomorrow would bring new challenges, new disappointments, and likely new pain. But for now, in the quiet darkness of his room, Hadie allowed himself to dream of a future where he could find acceptance, understanding, and perhaps even love – both from others and, most importantly, from himself.

CHAPTER FOUR

Vanessa's eyes widened as she looked up at Nancy. "I have two questions," she said softly, her voice tinged with a mix of curiosity and apprehension.

Nancy smiled gently, sensing the girl's unease. "Go ahead, sweetheart. You can ask me anything."

Vanessa hesitated, then blurted out, "Why did she curse God? He didn't do anything wrong." Her brow furrowed, struggling to understand.

Nancy's expression softened. She sat on the edge of the bed, placing a comforting hand on Vanessa's shoulder. "Oh, my dear child," she said with a sigh. "Sometimes, when people are in pain or confused, they lash out at God or even at others. It's not right, but it's a very human reaction when we're hurting and don't understand why."

Vanessa nodded slowly, processing this. After a moment, she asked her second question, her voice barely above a whisper: "Is the story real?"

Nancy shook her head, relieved to dispel this fear. "No, it isn't real. If it was, I certainly wouldn't have considered taking you all trick-or-treating tonight."

Anne, who had been listening intently, shuddered. "Real or not, it's the scariest story I've ever heard," she admitted, pulling her blanket tighter.

Lily, always quick with a tease, couldn't resist. "As old as you are, you're still scared?" But there was a hint of affection in her voice.

Mike, ever the peacemaker, chimed in. "We all have the right to be scared of something. It's okay, Anne."

Nancy stood up, her eyes twinkling with amusement. "You know, the funniest part is that the government actually renovated the so-called Storkinas' house just to make the story seem more real. Can you believe it?"

Lily's indignation flared. "What? They could do that, but they couldn't send us to school?" The bitterness in her voice was palpable, a reminder of the hardships they'd faced.

Nancy's smile faltered for a moment, her heart aching for these children she'd grown to love. "Well," she said, forcing cheer into her voice, "it's bedtime now, my darlings." She tucked them in, her touch lingering as she smoothed their blankets. Turning off the light, she whispered, "Goodnight, my loves," before gently closing the door.

In the darkness, Lily fumbled for her flashlight, determination etched on her young face. The others, sensing her movement, gathered around.

"What are you up to, Lily?" Mike asked, concern evident in his voice.

Lily hesitated, then admitted, "I'm planning something. I want to see if Melaangel is real."

Anne's face paled in the dim light. "Lily, no! That's too dangerous. I love you all too much to let you do this."

Vanessa, torn between curiosity and fear, spoke up. "But what if we could help her?"

Mike, always protective, warned, "If we do this, we can't touch her. We have to be careful."

As they debated, their voices a mix of excitement and trepidation, Anne felt a growing sense of dread. These were the only family she had left. The thought of losing them was unbearable.

"Please," she begged, her voice cracking. "Don't do this. We're all we have. Vanessa back me up here."

The others exchanged glances, the weight of Anne's words sinking in.

"Sorry, Anne, but she's right," Vanessa said breaking the silence.

"Mike, what about you? I know you won't let me down," Anne said.

"I would never," Mike said, "but neither would I let Lily down. If we do this, Melaangel would be happy," he added.

"How would you even know where she is? It's not like she'd be in the house they renovated," Anne said. Then a flickering light outside caught their attention. A billboard had appeared, as if by magic: 'Come experience the shock of your life. A being has been found in the Storkinas' home.'

The children stared, a mix of fear and exhilaration coursing through them. In that moment, childhood curiosity battled with very real fears, and the bonds of their makeshift family were about to be tested in ways they never imagined.

"Okay that sign is scary but see, it's there or she's there whichever" Vanessa said.

"How would we get there? We don't have money," Anne said as everyone looked at each other with a smile.

"What? What is it?" Anne asked.

"You could stay home and cover for us while we sneak there," Lily suggested.

"I can't," Anne said.

"Please, sis, do it for us," Mike pleaded.

"I can't," Anne repeated.

"I didn't want to do this, but twin promise," Mike said.

They all gasped.

"Why are we gasping?" Lily asked.

"He just used a twin promise. It can't be broken," Anne said.

"What's so special about that? Every promise can always be broken," Lily said.

"Well, if you were a twin, it can't," Anne said. "But you're going to have to get me something to pay for it," she added.

"Fine, what is it?" Mike asked.

"I want a pack of ice cream, extra-large," Anne said.

"But I don't have money," Mike said.

"Then I won't do it," Anne said.

"Fine, I will," Mike said as Anne went to Nancy's room, crying.

"Why are you crying? What happened?" Nancy asked.

"The story made me have bad dreams," Anne said.

"Okay, then you can sleep here. I'll watch you," Nancy said.

Meanwhile, the rest sneaked out.

"Now where are we to go? It's not like a sign will just appear saying 'follow here to go to the Storkinas' house,'" Vanessa said.

To Vanessa surprise a sign appeared: 'Follow here to the Storkinas' house.' They followed it and got there. Luckily, no one was there so they were able to sneak in unnoticed.

"Now, Mike, you keep guard," Lily said.

"Okay, this place is massive like a mansion" Mike agreed.

"One it is a mansion, two don't go anywhere Mike please our safety rest in your hand" Lily said

They entered into the building with Mike at the entrance, there was a long stairway ahead of them.

"Hello, anyone here?" Vanessa asked as Lily covered her mouth. "Do you want her to kill us?" Lily whispered.

A few minutes later, someone entered the place while he was distracted. "Who's there?" they shouted in fright. Then a man came from behind and grabbed them.

"Unhand me," Lily said.

"I'm taking you home," the man said. As they were being dragged, they saw Mike.

"Weren't you supposed to be keeping guard?" Vanessa asked.

"Yes, but this guy gave me money, enough for me to buy what Anne wanted," Mike said. They were dragged home.

A knock at the door. "Did you hear that?" Nancy asked.

"No, Nancy, we shouldn't go and check it out," Anne said. The knock continued.

"Okay, I have to check it out," Nancy said as Anne tried to stop her to no avail. Upon reaching the door, Nancy opened it.

"How can I help you, kind sirs?" Nancy asked.

"Well, we saw these rascals sneaking around the Storkinas' home," the man said.

"I'm so sorry about that. I promise it won't happen again," Nancy said as she took them in.

"Well, I hope so. You look like they could be in school," the man said.

"What did you say?" Nancy asked.

"Oh, sorry, I meant that they look like they could be in school," the man said.

"Oh yeah, they are supposed to be, but this is a foster home. They're not really my kids, and I can't afford school," Nancy said.

"Well, that's sad because I was wondering if we could maybe go out somewhere," the man said.

"You don't even know my name," Nancy said.

"Oops, my bad. I am Marc, and you must be..." the man said with a smile plastered on his face.

"Nice to meet you. I am Nancy, but I'm not really interested," she said.

"Oh, okay, I guess. See you next time, not," he said as he walked away.

"I can't believe you did that," Anne said.

"Don't change the topic. You guys went out without my consent," Nancy said.

"We're sorry. We just wanted to find out if she was real," Lily said.

"I said she wasn't, but you still insisted on going to look for answers. Well, that's not nice," Nancy said.

"Okay, we were wrong, and we're sorry. It was all my idea," Lily admitted.

"Well, I had news to tell you guys, but I guess it has to come now... You are starting school next week, Monday," Nancy said as they celebrated.

"Yes, we would find people to help us," Vanessa whispered.

"What did you say, Essa?" Nancy asked.

"Nothing," Vanessa replied.

"Now it's time for you to be asleep," Nancy said.

CHAPTER FIVE

The alarm rang at 6 AM, jolting Jalil from a deep sleep. He groaned, reluctantly turning off the persistent beeping, the sound echoing in the stillness of his room. Sunlight streamed through the window, casting a warm glow that contrasted sharply with the coolness of the early morning air. "It's time for school!" his mother called from downstairs, her voice filled with the energy of a new day.

"I'm on my way!" Jalil replied, rubbing the sleep from his eyes as he stood before the mirror. He pondered which shirt to wear, holding up two options. "Which dress says 'I love electronics'?" he mused, a playful smile creeping onto his face as he imagined the reactions of his classmates.

Minutes later, he was ready and hurried downstairs, the smell of toast and eggs wafting through the air, mingling with the faint scent of freshly brewed hot chocolate. "So, what are you planning today, Jalil?" his dad asked, seated at the dining table, a newspaper spread before him.

"Nothing much," Jalil replied, his mind already drifting to the day ahead.

"Let's go to school already!" his younger brother, Andrew, urged, his impatience palpable.

"Chill, little bro," Jalil said with a smile, appreciating the innocence of his brother's enthusiasm.

"Says the computer genius," Andrew teased, his eyes sparkling with mischief.

"Me? Nah, I'm still in training," Jalil chuckled, the warmth of family filling the room.

"Well, the bus is here," their mother announced, and the boys rushed out, the crisp morning air greeting them as they stepped outside.

"I love the smell of the school bus in the morning," Andrew said, grinning broadly.

"You're joking, right?" Jalil asked, raising an eyebrow.

"Of course I am! I was being sarcastic," Andrew replied, laughter bubbling between them as they boarded the bus.

As they arrived at the school entrance, the sight of vibrant decorations greeted them. "It's beautiful! That's what I would have said if I hadn't already seen the decorations," Andrew remarked, his voice filled with a mix of awe and familiarity.

"Well, bye! See you after torment!" he added, waving as he walked away, his carefree spirit a stark contrast to Jalil's more contemplative demeanour.

"Jalil! Jalil! Wait up!" Drake shouted from a distance, his voice cutting through the morning chatter. Jalil turned to see Drake sprinting toward him, his face lit up with excitement.

"Hey, yo, Drake! How are you doing?" Jalil asked as they shook hands, the warmth of their friendship palpable.

"You won't believe what happened!" Drake exclaimed, his eyes wide with anticipation.

"Let me guess: a girl asked you out?" Jalil replied sarcastically, a grin playing on his lips.

"I wish! No, my parents are going out this weekend, and I'm planning the most epic party!" Drake said, his excitement infectious.

"What are you celebrating?" Jalil asked, curiosity piqued.

"Well, it's just for fun," Drake replied, a mischievous glint in his eye. "There's going to be drinking, dancing, and many activities."

Jalil hesitated, a worried look crossing his face. "I have strict parents, so I can't come," he admitted, the weight of his reality settling in.

"Come on, you can sneak out, and we could maybe—" Drake started, but Jalil interrupted.

"I know we've been friends since high school started, and I really appreciate that, but no matter what I do, I'm not going to be accepted here because of my color," Jalil said, his voice heavy with emotion, the truth of his struggles surfacing.

"What makes you feel that way?" Drake asked, concern etching his features.

"For starters, I come from Africa, and I have different beliefs. I can't even explain it, but I could never..." Just then, the bell rang, signalling the start of class, and they hurried inside. A flashback of how their friendship was born plays in Jalil's mind from the first day of high school.

As Jalil walked through the bustling hallways, a group of students approached him, hurling insults that pierced through the lively chatter. Suddenly, Drake appeared from the shadows, stepping in to help.

"Leave him alone!" Drake shouted, his voice firm as he raised his fist in readiness to defend his friend.

"Fine, have him. After all, he's worthless here," the bully sneered, retreating with his group, leaving Jalil shaken but grateful for Drake's support.

"Hi, I'm Drake. Nice to meet you. You must be the new kid," he said, helping Jalil up from the floor, the kindness in his voice a balm for Jalil's bruised spirit.

"I'm Jalil. Thanks a lot. I guess not everyone is the same," Jalil replied, taking Drake's hand and standing up, a flicker of hope igniting within him.

At lunch, they sat together, the cafeteria buzzing with laughter and chatter. "Honestly, I feel like an outcast in everything," Jalil admitted, his voice barely above a whisper.

"I can tell," Drake said sympathetically, his gaze steady and understanding.

"Yes, Jalil?" the teacher called, noticing his hand raised. Jalil felt a rush of confusion, as if he had just won an unexpected award. "I... I... think the answer is..." he stammered, glancing at the board where they were discussing the figure of speech known as an oxymoron.

"It's a term used when two contradictory words are brought together simultaneously, like 'beautifully ugly,'" Jalil answered, and the teacher smiled at him, pride evident in her eyes.

After class, the teacher called him over. "Hope I'm not in trouble," Jalil said, his heart racing as he tried to recall what he might have done wrong.

"No, no, relax! I just wanted to tell you that you're doing well in my class. Any idea what you want to be?" she asked, her tone encouraging.

"Well, I'd like to be a programmer like Hadie," he said, his voice steady with determination.

"That's a nice choice," the teacher replied. "But you don't have to be like anyone else to show your worth," she added, her words resonating deeply with Jalil as she excused him from class.

At lunch, Jalil met up with Drake again. "What's up, Jalil? How was class?" Drake asked, his enthusiasm unwavering.

"Well, it was okay, I guess," Jalil said, his face expressionless, the weight of his earlier conversation lingering.

"I know what will cheer you up! How about a walk in the park?" Drake suggested, his eyes sparkling with the promise of adventure.

"That's like a million miles away from school," Jalil replied, a hint of skepticism in his voice.

"I didn't mean the one in town; I meant the one in school," Drake clarified, his laughter infectious.

"Oh yeah, I guess I was carried away," Jalil said, a smile breaking through as they walked through the bustling hallway, the sounds of laughter and chatter surrounding them.

"Did you ever wish that life would give you everything you want?" Jalil asked, his tone contemplative.

"Well, come to think of it, if it did, then no one would have a reason to live," Drake replied, his voice thoughtful.

"What about Adam and Eve?" Jalil countered, a hint of mischief in his eyes.

"Well," Drake began, "they had everything: a garden, peace, unity, love, smiles."

"Yeah, but it was because of them that we all have to suffer," Jalil said, a shadow crossing his face, the weight of history heavy on his heart.

Just then, the televisions in the hallway turned on, capturing their attention. "Are you feeling alone, unhappy, stressed out, tired of life, or confused? Well, look no further! Download the H.A.D.I.V.E. app and get a life-changing experience. Not only does it make life easier, but it's the only social media you'll ever need. So say goodbye to TikTok, Snapchat, and even that app called Facebook— or should I say Meta—and say hello to Happiness Amusement, De Friends Joiner app, Independent and Not Alone, Visual, Excitement, app H.A.D.I.V.E. It's designed to build bonds, not break them. Goodbye, and make sure you download it!"

the commercial blared, its bright colors and upbeat music contrasting sharply with the weight of the boys' conversation, a reminder of the complexities of life they were just beginning to navigate.

CHAPTER SIX

Nancy sighed as she looked around the cluttered living room of the foster home. Toys and books were strewn across the worn carpet, evidence of the lively children who called this place home. Sunlight streamed through the faded curtains, casting a warm glow on the mismatched furniture.

“What are we doing today, Nancy?” Vanessa asked. As she approached Nancy

Anne, always the mischievous one, couldn't resist teasing. "How about we call Nancy's boyfriend?" she suggested with a sly grin. The other children erupted into giggles, their laughter filling the room.

Lily, ever the responsible one, tried to redirect the conversation. "How about you go clean your rooms?" she suggested, her voice tinged with exasperation. At 16, she often felt caught between childhood and adulthood, struggling to find her place. Mike bristled at Lily's authoritative tone. "And who put you in charge?" he challenged, his voice cracking slightly. At 16, he was in the throes of adolescence, quick to assert his independence.

"Need I remind you that I am the eldest here?" Lily retorted, drawing herself up to her full height. The tension in the room was palpable as the two teens faced off.

"Just because you're a few months older doesn't mean you're in charge," Mike countered, his face flushing with anger. "Does too," Lily insisted.

"Does not," Mike replied, and they continued to argue until Nancy finally intervened.

As Lily and Mike continued their heated argument, Nancy felt a headache building behind her eyes. The constant bickering was wearing on her nerves. She took a deep breath, steeling herself to intervene.

"I was planning for us to see a movie," Nancy announced, her voice cutting through the noise. The children immediately fell silent, their faces lighting up with excitement. "But because of what happened yesterday, I won't," she finished firmly.

A chorus of protests erupted, with Anne's plea rising above the rest. "Please, Nancy, take us to the movie," she begged, her voice trembling with emotion.

The sudden knock at the door startled them all. Nancy's heart skipped a beat as she opened it to reveal Marc standing on the porch, his police uniform crisp and neat. His warm smile sent a flutter through her chest, despite her reservations. "I wonder who it could be," Nancy said as she got up to answer it. Upon opening the door, she was surprised. "Oh, hi Marc," Nancy greeted.

"Hi Nancy, nice to see you. How has your day been?" Marc asked.

"It's been alright, but I wasn't expecting you to come," Nancy replied.

"I couldn't help overhearing your argument," Marc said. "How about I give you guys a ride?"

"Well..." Nancy hesitated.

"Yes!" Anne interrupted, eager for the outing.

"That's okay, let's go then," Marc said, leading them to his Minivan.

Nancy held Anne back. "What is your problem? He could be a criminal or something," Nancy whispered.

"Well, we want to see a movie, and he offered us a ride. Besides, if he were a criminal, he would have kidnapped the children he found," Anne reasoned.

"Fair point," Nancy conceded.

"And what's wrong with having a police officer as a boyfriend?" Anne asked.

"I don't like him," Nancy said.

"That's how girls are; we like hiding our feelings. Honestly, if I liked a boy, I'd watch him first before dating him," Anne said.

"What do you know about boys? You were just nine when you and your brother arrived here," Nancy questioned.

"Well, I have a twin brother, and he likes a girl here but is too scared to tell her. But Marc was brave enough to ask you on a date, and when you pushed him away, he still came to help," Anne said as Mike came in to draw their attention back to the situation at hand.

"We'll be there in a minute," Anne said, holding Nancy's hand. "Whatever makes you feel he's not the one, then okay, listen to it, but give him a chance first," she added.

"That's not the issue; there's something else…" Nancy began, but was interrupted by Lily, who came to get their attention.

"Guys, please hurry up," Lily urged, and they finally left for the Minivan.

Marc started the vehicle, and they began moving. "This is such a big car," Mike said.

"Can you tell us about yourself?" Anne asked.

"Anne!" Nancy exclaimed.

"Don't worry, I can share. Well, for starters, I was an orphan too," Marc began.

"How did you become what you are?" Mike asked.

"Did you ever give up?" Lily inquired.

"Were you too lonely?" Anne asked.

"How did you cope?" Vanessa added, all at once, until Marc stopped them.

"Chill, calm down. I know you all have a lot of questions, but let me start my story," he said. "I was just six when I lost my parents. Things were hard because everyone thought I was a devil child, so I was segregated from the crowd. No friends, no one to talk to. Then I made up my mind that if I didn't try, nothing would change. I eventually went to a foster home and started exercising on my own until I was 18. When I had to move out because I became an adult, I decided to work as a police officer to help people. But I couldn't do that right away, so I first worked at a company called HARDIVE. I was able to earn enough money to finish school, and now I'm a junior officer since I'm still 27."

"Then how do you know... what, never mind," Mike said.

"I'm the assistant manager of HARDIVE, if you must know. That's why I'm helping you," Marc added.

Meanwhile, at the HQ of HARDIVE, Hadie was on a mission. "We need to find her," Hadie said.

"Isn't she your aunt?" one of the assistants asked.

"Actually, she might still be young, but if I was to calculate the age, she should be 80 by now," Hadie responded.

"And her powers are death," another assistant noted.

"I don't care; I want her," Hadie insisted. He approached the security guard monitoring the cameras. "How's your job going?" Hadie asked.

"It's going great, thanks for asking," the security guard replied.

"I wasn't talking to you, idiot. I was talking to Marc," Hadie said. "Well, he has surely gotten one thing, and that's them in his truck."

"That's alright. Once I get her, then I can scan her for the gene," Hadie said.

"You're her descendant; why don't you just use yourself?" the guard asked.

"It won't work. I've tried, and secondly, she is not. I was just saying it in high school so no one would bully me again, and this app I created has given me the recognition I deserve," Hadie said, then left for his office.

The witch appeared when Hadie was in his office. "Yes, what do you want?" Hadie asked.

"Well, nothing much, just what I asked for in return for the fame I gave you," the witch said.

"Well, I'm on it," Hadie replied.

"I know you're looking for Melaangel, but I can tell you that you will never find her. Just give me what you owe me, or you die," the witch threatened.

Hadie laughed, but then she made his hand paralyzed. "Okay, okay, please stop. I will, but let me just find her first," Hadie pleaded.

"Then you have until the 31st of October," the witch said.

"Thank you, at least I have a year to find her," Hadie said.

"No, you have until this October," the witch corrected.

"But I need more time," Hadie protested as she left.

"Fine, I need him to hurry up," Hadie said as he called Marc.

CHAPTER SEVEN

Marc Phone rings due to the fact it was on silent he only felt the vibration, he told Nancy and the others to excuse him he had to take the call from his boss.

"Hello, boss," Marc said as he Answered the phone call from Hadie's office.

"Well, how is the situation going?" Hadie asked, looking up from his desk.

"They are at the movie, boss," Marc reported.

Hadie's fingers tapped an impatient rhythm on the sleek surface of his desk. "We need to speed things up," he instructed, his tone leaving no room for argument.

A knot formed in Marc's stomach as he asked, "Why, boss?"

"Well, if you don't, you might get fired," Hardie replied bluntly, the threat hanging heavy in the air between them.

"Okay, I will," Marc said, nodding in understanding.

Later, as the sun dipped below the horizon, casting long shadows across the foster home's weathered porch, Marc stood at Nancy's door. His heart raced, palms sweating, nervously fidgeting. as he gathered his courage. "I was wondering if maybe you'd like to go out with me," he asked, his voice wavering slightly crossing his fingers in hopes she would say yes.

Nancy's eyes softened, a small smile playing at the corners of her mouth. "Well, I really had a nice day, and you were quite funny, so I guess I would go out with you," she replied, her words sending a surge of warmth through Marc's chest.

"Great! We could go to the mall," Marc suggested.

"How about next week? I have some things I want to do first," Nancy said.

"Okay, that's alright," Marc said, feeling relieved as Marc walked back to his Minivan, the gravel crunching beneath his feet, he felt a mix of elation and dread. The rusted metal of his truck door creaked as he opened it, a stark reminder of the simple life he longed for, so different from the sleek world of HARDIVE.

Nancy closed the door, placing her hand on her chest, feeling a mix of excitement and nervousness the worn floorboards creaked beneath her feet as she made her way to the living room, the familiar sounds and scents of home grounding her amidst the whirlwind of emotions. Meanwhile, Anne, who had been spying, rushed to tell the others.

"Yes! Now we can have time to find Melaangel!" Vanessa exclaimed.

Meanwhile, at Drake's house, in Drake's cluttered bedroom, posters of rock bands and action movies covering every inch of wall space, he grappled with his concerns for Jalil. The air was thick with the scent of unwashed laundry and stale pizza, a testament to teenage life. he was lost in thought, talking to himself. "Why is Jalil like this? He just holds himself back from having fun. What's his issue?"

"Have you tried convincing his parents?" his older sister, Freda, chimed in. Her presence a reminder of the thin walls and lack of privacy in their modest home.

"Hey! I thought no one was here! Wait a sec—Freda, what the hell are you doing in my room?" Drake asked, surprised.

"I heard you talking to yourself, so I decided to join the conversation. Have you tried convincing his parents? Most times, people feel the way they do because they're scared to face the consequences," Freda suggested.

"That's a good idea, but he feels that if we get in trouble, his punishment would be worse because of his color," Drake replied thoughtfully.

"He needs to be more open-minded," Freda said.

"Thanks, sis. You're the best," Drake said appreciatively.

"You're welcome. Now please leave my room; I have party guests to invite," Freda said, heading out.

At the HARDIVE headquarters, Marc reported back to Hadie. "We are going on a date," Marc said, trying to sound upbeat.

"Good," Hadie replied, but then added, "But it's next week."

"What?!" Hadie exclaimed, his frustration evident. "You better get on with it fast, or else you're fired."

"Why do you want her so badly? It's not like she could give you what you desire," Marc questioned.

"But she can lead us to the location with some testing," Hadie insisted.

"Okay, but promise me you won't hurt her," Marc said, his concern for Nancy clear.

"Fine, I promise," Hadie said, rolling his eyes. "Now go get ready. We have a long week ahead of us."

CHAPTER EIGHT

As the sun rose over the small town, a warm glow filled the foster home, illuminating the kitchen where Nancy was preparing breakfast. The scent of pancakes wafted through the air, mingling with the sound of laughter and chatter from the children as they eagerly anticipated their first day at school.

"I can't believe we're finally going to school! All the new friends I can make!" Vanessa exclaimed, her voice bubbling with excitement. Her bright eyes sparkled with dreams of new beginnings, reflecting a childlike innocence that made Nancy smile. "Seriously, is that the only thing that bothers you?" Anne teased, rolling her eyes but unable to hide her own enthusiasm. "Well, I still love you guys, but I want to meet other people," Vanessa replied in a sweet but sassy tune.

"Yeah, Vanessa is right. They could help us with our quest," Lily added as she packs her bag.

Meanwhile, Nancy felt a mix of anticipation and anxiety as she prepared for her date with Marc. She glanced at the clock, her heart racing at the thought of stepping into a new chapter of her life. Just as she finished setting the table, a knock echoed through the hallway.

"Coming!" she called out, her voice slightly shaky as she approached the door.

Opening it, she was greeted by Marc's warm smile, which instantly made her feel at ease. "Oh, hi Marc, nice to see you," she greeted him, her heart fluttering slightly.

"Yeah, what a lovely day to go shopping," Marc said. "That's if you still want to go or maybe change location."

"Well, I think we could just go to the mall first," Nancy suggested, her excitement bubbling beneath the surface.

"But first, let's drop off the kids at school," Marc proposed.

"That would be nice," Nancy agreed, her heart swelling with gratitude for his thoughtfulness.

Once the kids were ready, they piled into Marc's truck, the vehicle filled with laughter and chatter as they drove to school. The familiar streets of their neighbourhood passed by, each turn a reminder of the life they were building together. Upon arriving at the school, the principal welcomed them with open arms. "Welcome, new students!" he said warmly, his smile radiating kindness.

"Thanks, we are delighted to have this opportunity," Nancy replied.

"You can get going. I'll help them fit in," the principal assured her as he called Reece. Nancy and Marc left once Reece arrived.

"New students, how delightful! I would love to show you around," Reece said.

"Yes, a new friend, and he's kind of quiet," Vanessa noted as they followed him.

However, as they approached the janitor's closet, Reece's demeanour shifted. "As you look to your right, this is the class for new students," he said, pointing to the door marked with a faded sign.

"But it says, 'Janitor's Closet,'" Mike pointed out.

"Don't let that distract you. It's a class," Reece insisted, a hint of mischief in his voice as he led them inside. Before they could react, he closed the door and blocked it, leaving them in darkness.

"Hey, let us out of here!" Anne shouted, panic rising in her voice. "I knew he couldn't be trusted."

“What are we going to do now?” Mike asked, his voice trembling with uncertainty.

“Boys are jerks. How could he be good-looking but heartless?” Vanessa lamented, frustration evident in her tone.

“Hey!” Mike exclaimed defensively.

“Never mind that, we need to get out of here,” Lily said, her voice firm despite the fear creeping in.

Just then, Jalil and Drake approached, their expressions a mix of concern and curiosity. “I heard it coming from this direction,” Jalil said, looking around.

“What about the party? You had a lot of fun, right?” Drake asked, trying to lighten the mood.

“Yes, but we have a situation here right now,” Jalil replied. urgency in his tone.

“Okay, let’s go,” Drake said, leading them to the janitor’s closet. With a swift motion, Jalil opened the door, and the kids who were leaning against it tumbled out.

“Ouch,” Lily said as Jalil, and Drake helped them up.

“And that is why you don’t rest on the door,” Mike quipped, trying to inject humour into the tense situation.

"Ha-ha, very funny, Mike," Anne said, rolling her eyes but unable to suppress a smile.

"Let me guess, Reece locked you guys in here, right?" Drake asked.

"Yeah, he did," Vanessa confirmed.

"Welcome to the club, then," Jalil said, a hint of camaraderie forming in the air.

"What do you mean by that?" Lily asked, her curiosity piqued

"He locked me in there on my first day. I thought he was racist, but it appears he's just a jerk," Jalil explained, his voice laced with a mix of frustration and understanding.

"How about we introduce ourselves? I'm Derek, but you can call me Drake because I prefer that, and this is Jalil," Drake said, extending his hand with a friendly smile. "Oh, handsome," Vanessa whispered under her breath as she shook his hand, her cheeks flushing slightly.

"I'm Mike, the leader," Mike declared, but his sisters interrupted.

"No way! No one calls you that," Anne interjected, her tone teasing. "I'm Anne, by the way, his twin sister."

"Boldness, that's nice," Drake said quietly, impressed by her spirit.

"And I'm Vanessa, and this is Lily," Vanessa added, her voice brightening the atmosphere.

Jalil asked, genuinely curious.

"No, we're not, but we've lived together for quite some time, so I guess we could be," Lily said, her smile warm and inviting.

Just then, the bell rang, echoing through the hallways and signalling the start of their new adventure. "Oops, we need to go," Jalil said, trying to drag Drake with him.

"Chill," Drake replied, shaking his head. "We could meet up at the canteen after school."

"That's alright," Mike agreed.

"But we don't know the way to our classes," Lily said.

"Well, we could meet the receptionist," Jalil suggested.

"Yes, thanks," Vanessa said, clutching Drake's arm.

As they made their way through the bustling school, the energy of the students around them buzzed with excitement and anticipation, mirroring their own hopes for the future. Each step felt like a leap into the unknown, filled with both fear and exhilaration, as they navigated the complexities of friendship, trust, and the quest for belonging.

CHAPTER NINE

At the reception, Drake approached the desk. "We need directions to the classroom," he said.

"Not again, Drake. You know your class," the receptionist replied.

"Not for me, for her," Drake clarified, pointing to Vanessa, who was still holding his hand.

"Okay," the receptionist said as she checked the records after asking for their information. "You all are in the same class, and also take this to class to avoid punishment," she added, handing Vanessa a slip. Vanessa took it and finally let go of Drake's hand.

After school, Anne asked if they could go to the library. "Why?" Drake inquired.

"I want to research something," Anne replied.

"Okay, I could take you there," Drake offered.

"Thanks, that would be nice," Anne said.

"Can't all of us just go then?" Jalil asked.

"Of course," Anne agreed, though Drake gave Jalil a look.

"What's the issue?" Jalil asked.

"You know I wanted time alone with her," Drake said.

"Chill, I didn't know, and besides, we could help," Jalil said. "Don't tell me you've forgotten about your bestie incident."

"That was a mistake," Drake admitted with confidence and pride "Besides not like it can happen again" He added patting Jalil at the back.

"Okay, let's just go," Jalil said to everyone as they headed to the library.

"What are we looking for?" Drake asked.

"We need to find the book that tells us about Melaangel," Lily said.

"I've heard about that. My parents told me about it," Drake said.

"Cool, what did they say?" Anne asked.

"She is a witch with a curse who comes out on Halloween day and kills anyone she is not pleased with," Drake explained.

"That's not cool, It's so scary" Anne said as she pretends to be scared. "I wonder who would tell their kids that?" She added

"My parents hated me going out for trick or treating so they find ways to stop me" Drake explained.

"Okay, let's start looking," Jalil said.

They searched for several hours and were about to give up. "How did we not find it?" Anne asked.

Jalil came rushing to the group with a book in his hand "I found it," Jalil said just as they were losing hope.

"Seriously, let me see," Anne said as she took the book. "It says 'Temple of Death.' This is not it," she said, tossing the book on the table. It fell open to a page about Melaangel.

"No way," they all exclaimed.

"It says she is not a god, just a human cursed with an enchanted spell by her mother because of the way her family was treated. Her father was treated the worst and was later killed after her mother's death, but she was nowhere to be found. It also says the curse cannot be removed," Lily read aloud.

"What does her name mean?" Jalil asked.

"Melaangel means 'angel of death,'" Anne said.

"I see," Jalil said.

"What do you mean?" Vanessa asked.

"I have no idea; I just say it," Jalil replied.

"Yeah, he says it a lot," Drake added.

"How are we going to find her?" Lily asked.

"It didn't say so," Mike said.

"Wait a sec, you guys are going to find her?" Jalil asked.

"Yes, we want to help her," Anne said.

"How?" Jalil asked.

"We have no idea; we just want to help her," Vanessa said.

"At least they talk like me before, but I have changed. There is always a cure for everything," Anne said.

"I think we should be going home," Jalil said as he and Drake left.

Meanwhile, after Marc and Nancy had finished their outing, they realized the kids had finished school. "Oh, wait, we have people that have closed for school," Nancy said.

"Oh yeah," Marc said as he held her hand, and they went to the truck to pick them up.

Later at home, Marc and Nancy talked, and most of the time, Nancy was laughing. In their room, Anne, who was spying, went to her siblings. "Yes, this would be easy with Nancy distracted. We have a trail; we can finally find her," Anne said.

"But we saw nothing in the book," Vanessa said.

"Have you forgotten the title? It says 'Temple of Death.' That's obviously where she would be," Anne said.

"And how would we find it?" Mike asked.

"Well, Lily," Anne said as Lily brought out a device.

"Wow, what is that for?" Vanessa asked.

"Years ago, Lily and I realized that Nancy always reads us the same story, and it implies she has a family mission to accomplish. Everyone from Abel's lineage has to know and read the book. I know I'm not getting anywhere, but I can tell you this: Nancy is from her lineage, so we can use her DNA to track the exact location of Melaangel," Anne explained.

"And you guys never told us?" Vanessa asked.

"Well, if we did, it wouldn't be a Halloween surprise, would it?" Lily said.

"I don't understand. Then why did you want the book in the library?" Mike asked.

"I knew that the Storkinas wouldn't want the witch to know they have a location, so they hid it in invisible ink, which I knew you guys wouldn't believe exists," Anne said.

"Tomorrow we are going to have a hike," Mike said.

"But Nancy would realize we're gone," Vanessa said.

"We've got it covered," Lily said as she showed off her robot impressions of them. "I got it with the HARDIVE app. It's super cool."

They then went to bed, and a few minutes later, Nancy came to check on them.

CHAPTER TEN

The morning after their initial conversation, Anne and her foster family gathered together for breakfast, her excitement conspicuous.

"Nancy, when you finish work, we'd like to go to the library and catch up on what we've missed so far at school. Is that okay with you?" Anne asked, her fork poised over her plate.

Nancy smiled warmly, arranging plates of steaming pancakes drizzled with syrup. "I don't see why not. It's good to see you all so eager to study."

"Thanks, Nancy," Lily chimed in, her voice tinged with a mix of excitement and guilt. She knew the real motive behind their library visit could spell trouble if discovered.

As the day unfolded, Marc arrived to drive everyone to school. The air buzzed with chatter and laughter as they piled into the van, a sense of camaraderie enveloping them.

"Early as usual," Nancy remarked affectionately, giving Marc a peck on the cheek.

Marc blushed, his eyes softening. "It's no biggie," he replied.

As they neared the school, Nancy lowered the car window, her tone shifting to one of maternal concern. "Don't take too much time in the library, okay? We might not be able to come back to pick you up, so please come straight home." They all nodded at once to show they agree with what Nancy has said.

“Why are you guys still standing here,” Vanessa asked, “The school is right there” she said walking off leaving the rest behind.

“I wonder where she is rushing too,” Anne said

“You should know by now” Mike said with a smirk.

Later after 3 hours of boring lectures it was finally break, Anne and the Gang Gathered round a table where they have sat ready to eat but, Anne chimes in,

“Guys, guess what?” Anne said excitedly.

“What?” Jalil asked.

"We're going on a trip," Anne announced, her words hanging in the air like a promise of freedom.

Drake's face lit up with excitement, while Jalil's brow furrowed with worry. "But I'm not ready," he protested, his voice quavering slightly.

"Oh yeah, that's true. His parents don't let him do anything fun," Drake added, his words unintentionally stinging Jalil.

Lily, sensing Jalil's discomfort, quickly interjected. "I've got that covered," she said, gesturing to a pair of robots resembling Drake and Jalil.

"Cool," Drake said.

"Can it function like me?" Jalil asked.

"It can do better than you," Lily teased.

"Then I'm in," Jalil said, "Although how come you can build a bot but you never told us" Jalil said with a doubt.

"Jalil no," she said laughing, "I got it from Hardive" Lily said

"Nice, after school, we leave," Anne said.

At the closing bell they all met up at the entrance of the school,

"We would be going now" Anne announced with excitement.

"Wait but we aren't ready" Drake said.

"Seriously guys there is an app for that" Lily said as she ordered clothes for them, they began their journey.

"How long will it take?" Jalil asked.

"At most, two days," Anne replied.

Jalil fright began to creep in the more, "Two days" He exclaimed

"Okay, let's go to... where exactly are we going?" Drake asked, shifting the attention from Jalil.

"To the Temple of Death," Lily said as they journeyed onward.

"I wonder what it would be like to actually find her," Anne mused.

"I feel it would be awesome because we'd be the only ones to ever find her location," Mike said.

"That is so true. I could give myself a pat on the back," Vanessa added as they walked for miles. Finally, they reached a spot, and as it was getting dark, they had to find somewhere to shelter.

"I brought tents. We could set them up over there," Lily suggested, pointing to an area with minimum grasses and rocks.

Meanwhile, at home, Nancy was talking with Marc. "Would you like to come to my workplace? I'd love to show you where I work," Marc suggested.

"I thought you were a guard," Nancy said.

"Yes, I was, but now I work with the richest company ever," Marc explained.

"That's nice. I would love to," Nancy said.

"Okay, see you tomorrow then," Marc said.

Meanwhile, at the campfire, Mike had a suggestion. "Who would like to tell us a story so we can get closer to each other?" he asked.

"Hmm," Anne pondered.

"How about spin the bottle?" Vanessa suggested, pulling out a bottle.

"That sounds better," everyone agreed as she spun the bottle, and it pointed at Drake.

"Now, Drake, what is your favourite colour?" Vanessa asked.

"My favourite colour is yellow because it's the colour of the sun when it shines bright like the smile of an angel," Drake answered flirtingly.

"Aww," Vanessa said.

"Actually, we are hunting for an angel," Mike joked trying to steal the spotlight.

"That was so not funny," Vanessa said with a straight face as Lily giggled. Then Lily spun the bottle, and it landed on Jalil.

"Alright, what is your worst nightmare?" Lily asked, but Jalil just left and sat on a rock. Drake followed him.

"What's wrong?" Drake asked gently.

"Nothing," Jalil replied, avoiding eye contact.

"Don't tell me nothing," Drake insisted, sitting beside him.

"Well, I'm not really a 'girl's kind of guy.' Almost anything I say could be a crime, so I can't take that chance. It feels odd for me to be here. But I can't stay home bored while my friends are on an adventure," Jalil admitted, his voice barely above a whisper. "My sister told me that you should stop looking down on yourself," Drake said, trying to encourage him.

"Wow, I've become a topic for you guys," Jalil joked, attempting to lighten the mood.

"Not really. As your best friend, I want to help you feel like you belong, so you stop treating yourself like an outcast. I'm an outcast too," Drake said, sincerity in his voice.

"I guess I do that a lot, but I'll take your advice," Jalil said, returning to the campfire.

"My worst nightmare is never being accepted," Jalil confessed, vulnerability in his eyes.

"Don't worry, we'll always be here for you," Mike reassured him as rain began to fall.

"It's time we go inside," Lily said, sensing the change in weather.

The next day, Nancy prepared to go out with Marc but noticed that Anne and her friends had already left for school. "That's nice; at least now we can go to his office on time," she said to herself as she walked out the door, not noticing Marc leaning against his car.

"Who are you talking about?" Marc asked, startling Nancy.

"Let's just go," she said, taking his hand, her heart racing with anticipation.

"Maybe we could go somewhere else," Marc suggested, a glint of mischief in his eyes.

"I thought we were going to your workplace," Nancy replied, intrigued.

"Yeah, we are. I just have somewhere I'd love to show you," Marc said, excitement bubbling over.

"Okay, no problem," Nancy agreed, curiosity piqued. "Where is it?" she asked as he opened the door for her to get in the passenger seat of his minivan.

Marc rushed to the other side and climbed in, adjusting his seat before starting the vehicle. "It's a surprise," he said, a playful smile on his face as they drove off into the unknown.

CHAPTER ELEVEN

As dawn broke, the group emerged from their tents, ready to continue their journey. Jalil, showing newfound confidence, took charge. "Let's pack up and move out," he said, his voice carrying a hint of excitement.

Mike, fidgeting with a folded note, approached Vanessa. "Hey, I've been wanting to tell you something," he said, his voice wavering slightly. "I'll understand if you don't feel the same way, but could you read this?" He handed her the note, his heart pounding.

Vanessa took the note, a mix of curiosity and apprehension in her eyes. "Thanks, I'll read it later. We should focus on packing up for now," she replied, tucking the note away.

As they trekked for hours, the group's dynamics shifted. Vanessa approached Mike, Drake, and Jalil, her expression serious. "Drake, I'm sorry, but I don't think this can work between us," she said gently

Drake nodded in confusion, his face a mask of misunderstanding. "Okay," he replied simply.

“Mike, my answer is yes,” Vanessa said as she held Mike’s hand, and they walked away together.

Jalil looked at Drake, confusion evident in his eyes. "You broke up with Vanessa?"

Drake shrugged, a wry smile on his face. "We never even dated, she just kept acting like we were and I didn’t mind cause I was just trying to be nice."

“If you say so,” Jalil said patting Drake’s back.

Drake said with a smile, “I saw him writing a lot of notes but I pretend to be asleep, I opened one and I knew what was going to happen although I didn’t expect him to have to have the courage to do so,” He said as they both laugh.

“Alright, let’s just continue,” Jalil added, his tone pragmatic as they neared the temple.

A few hours later, they reached the temple entrance. “Now we have reached our destination,” Lily announced as they walked into the temple.

“I’ll be honest Temples are meant to be in a sandy environment?” Drake asked

“Yeah” Lily answered.

“But this place is like two days away from the city.” Drake said

“I wonder if there are traps because normally there are supposed to be traps,” Anne said shifting attention from Drake.

As they cautiously entered, Anne voiced her concerns. "I wonder if there are traps. There are usually traps in places like this."

Despite their careful steps, no traps were triggered, and the temple seemed eerily empty.

"Well, this is a relief. Nothing's here," Mike said, his voice echoing in the cavernous space.

Vanessa leaned into him, her voice soft. "But I am here for you," she said as they shared a kiss.

Anne, growing impatient, urged them on. "Okay, guys, let's go." But as she spoke, they inadvertently triggered a trap. The ground beneath them began to crumble.

"Oh no," Lily gasped, her eyes wide with fear.

"What's 'oh no'?" Jalil asked, panic rising in his voice.

"We're going to be crushed, and the exit is already blocked," Lily explained, her mind racing for a solution.

Suddenly, the floor gave way, and they found themselves sliding down a hidden passage, emerging outside the temple.

"Thank God we're alive," Jalil said with a sigh of relief.

A mysterious voice cut through their moment of respite. "You were lucky," it said. They turned to see Melaangel standing before them.

Anne's eyes lit up with recognition. "Oh wow, it's her," she said, moving towards Melaangel. Drake quickly pulled her back.

"Have you forgotten she can kill with a touch?" Drake reminded her, his voice tense.

Anne smiled confidently. "No need to worry, I've got it covered," she said, producing a pair of gloves. "These will prevent you from killing people with your touch," she explained to Melaangel. "You can come with us now."

Melaangel's eyes filled with sadness. "Thanks, but I can't. I have no memory of my past. All I know is that I kill when anyone I love is hurt."

“What if we change your name?” Lily suggested.

“How is that going to help?” Anne asked.

“Did you never pay attention to the story when Nancy reads to us, it said the son Abel should find her and change her name" Lily said with all confidence sure that her research was worth the try.

"Yeah if that's so it happened in the Bible, a guy named Saul loved to kill Christians, but his name was changed to Paul, and he became a better person," Jalil explained.

"Wow, I never thought of that," Melaangel said. "That's the dumbest idea I have ever heard."

"How" Jalil asked with confusion.

"Firstly those people are not me and I never had a younger brother, also In the bible Saul was blind and he had to repent in other to get his sight back, look at me what sin did I commit to be the one with this curse" Melaangel said in frustration "You guys should just leave please I don't want to kill you guys or anyone that's why I hid in this temple away from everyone" she said as tears filled her eyes.

"So you are telling me I came here for no reason" Drake said in frustration

"It's alright Drake let's just go she doesn't want to come with us" Anne said sadly.

"I can't believe this" Lily said with frustration throwing her book on the ground.

"I won't leave not yet" Drake said as he faces Melaangel "You, you are a real devil, you killed people fine, we didn't care about that Lily and Anne all spent their life hoping they could find you and help you but here you are being an ungrateful being telling us to go back that we wasted two days for no reason" Drake said in annoyance and they start to walk back. Melaangel Faced head down then she looks up and shouts out "Guys," they all face back, "I'm sorry for what I said let's give it a try please" Melaangel said as she walked towards them.

"How about we name her Deborah?" Jalil proposed.

"Deborah, I like it. From now on, I will be called Deborah," she said as a dust wave spread. Making the gloves on her hand Vanish. she then touched a plant to test it, but the plant died.

"At least we tried." Anne said.

"Anyone hungry, Let's go and order pizza," Drake said

"Pizza? I haven't tasted that in a while because food I touch disintegrates," Deborah said as she approached an abandoned car. "Even Vehicles as well"

"How would we get home now?" Vanessa asked.

Deborah then touched the car, and it started working. "No way" Deborah said in excitement

They hopped in, and she drove them to the nearest restaurant while using google maps. A few hours later they arrived in the city

"I'm happy we found her, but I guess I have to go home. Bye," Jalil said as he left with Drake.

"I have an idea, and it might not work, but I have to try," Jalil said as they headed home.

Meanwhile, Mike and his friends snuck Deborah into the house and goes to their room.

"We need to understand how it worked I mean to make the car actually start again that's like the opposite of death," Lily said. Unknown to them Nancy was in their room cause she got a report from the school that they haven't been in school for days. "Why haven't you been in school for two days and who is she?" Nancy asked

"You see," Lily begins "We went to find her" She said pointing at Deborah

"Who is she?" Nancy asked

"This is Deborah aka Melaangel" Anne said

"That's a lie," Nancy said doubting "Prove it" she added

Deborah decided to share her story. "My dad was an African who believed strongly in God, but my mum was the opposite. Because of that, my mum went to a witch for a child, and in return, I was cursed so that anyone who threatened any of my family members would die."

"That proves nothing" Nancy said as she notices Vanessa and Mike smiling awkwardly.

"What's got you two pumped up?" Nancy asked

"Mike and I are dating," Vanessa said.

"Wow that sounds rushed" Nancy mocked

"Hey, that's not fair, I was literally fidgeting when I gave her the note" Mike said

"Really a note, how old are you?" Nancy asked

"It doesn't matter I love him and he loves me" Vanessa said

"I'm joking with you guys, but the part about you missing school for two days and coming back with a stranger is no fair what if her family is looking for her" Nancy said

"We can leave her here till her family comes then" Lily suggested.

"Alright, but you would all still be punished" Nancy said as she leaves but comes back cause she forgot the main reason she came there, "I'm going to Marc's office tomorrow. Just wanted to be sure you guys would be alright going to school without our help," Nancy said.

"That's okay," Anne said.

"And we would accept our punishment" Lily said.

"Alright then, I'll leave you guys to do whatever you want to do," Nancy said as she left.

The next day, Deborah dropped them off at school. "You can follow us; you look our age,". Lily said.

"Okay," Deborah agreed and followed them.

Later on, at lunch, Jalil who gave Lily a note before class approached Lily. "What do you think about my letter?" he asked.

"Oh, that. I guess we could be just friends," Lily replied.

"Okay," Jalil said, then left.

"Where do you think he's going?" Lily asked.

"I'll go after him," Drake said as he followed Jalil.

"Let me guess, you were trying it out, right?" Drake asked.

"Yeah, but I knew it was a dumb idea, yet I still tried," Jalil admitted.

"At least you guys are still friends," Drake said.

"You know what? That's not bad after all," Jalil said.

"Hey, what happened to the old Jalil?" Drake asked.

"Well, he has taken a hike," Jalil said.

"I like this new Jalil," Drake said.

Meanwhile, at the headquarters, Hadie was plotting. "Yes, this is great. Once I'm done with my test, I'll be able to locate Melaangel, and then that stupid witch can give me more power," Hadie said.

"What exactly is she going to do with Nancy?" Marc asked.

"That's not my problem," Hadie said.

"But you promised not to hurt her," Marc reminded him.

"When have you seen someone who wants power keep their promise? But I hope she's not completely drained," Hadie said as he called out to the guards, who then threw Marc out of the HQ.

CHAPTER TWELVE

As the sun went to sleep and silence dawn on the city Deborah drove up the driveway of their house, on exciting the car and opening the door they see everything in disarray.

“I wonder what happened here” Vanessa mused, her voice tinged with concern. “Maybe a tornado I always experience that in the temple” Debby suggested, recalling similar experiences from her time at the temple.

"How about we get some rest and tackle this mess tomorrow?" Lily proposed, stifling a yawn. Everyone nodded in agreement, their fatigue outweighing their curiosity.

Meanwhile at Jalil’s house he is greeted with his dad who came home early from work today and is confronting Jalil.

"What? You haven't been in school for two days?" Jalil's father confronted him, holding up his phone with a recording of a call from Jalil's teacher.

"Are you calling your teacher a liar?" his mother interjected, her tone sharp.

"Fine, I went out with my friends to find something historical," Jalil admitted, his shoulders slumping under the weight of his confession.

"With whose permission?" his mother pressed, her eyes narrowing.

"The only reason you're not in more trouble is because I'm in a good mood today," his father added, his voice a mix of sternness and understanding.

"It's not that we're against you going out with your friends," his mother continued, her voice softening. "We just want you to be careful."

"I'm sorry," Jalil apologized, his eyes meeting his parents' as they exchanged a silent conversation.

"You're the eldest," his father finally said, his voice firm but gentle. "You need to set a good example for your siblings. Promise me you'll behave responsibly."

Jalil hesitated, the weight of his father's words sinking in. Finally, he nodded. "I promise."

The next day at school, Jalil shared his ordeal with Drake.

"My parents found out I wasn't in school," Jalil said, a hint of relief in his voice.

Drake gasped. "What did they say?"

"They were calmer than I expected," Jalil replied, a small smile playing on his lips.

Their conversation was abruptly interrupted as Anne, Deborah, Vanessa, and a couple of others rushed toward them, their voices a cacophony of panic.

"The house was a mess!"

"Nancy is missing!"

"The robots are evil!"

"Calm down," Jalil urged, raising his hands to quiet them. "We can't understand you if you're all talking at once."

CHAPTER THIRTEEN

After Jalil was able to make them settle down they spoke one by one "Okay, first of all, we didn't see Nancy this morning," Anne explained, her voice trembling with urgency. "We discovered the robots tore down the house, and we kept hearing this strange humming sound." She added

"We need to find her. We can't live without her," Lily added, her eyes wide with worry.

"Sorry, guys, but I can't help. My parents already found out," Jalil said, regret heavy in his voice.

"Oh no," Lily gasped.

"What is wrong?" Jalil asked, sensing her distress.

"Your parents might be in danger," Anne said, her voice barely above a whisper.

"How do you guys know all this and never tell us?" Mike demanded, frustration creeping into his tone.

“Your too dumb to understand” Lily teased.

“Hėy stop that” Venessa defended him

"Well, at the cinema, I saw Marc making a call. He mentioned a robot attack on the 31st," Anne admitted, guilt washing over her.

"And you stayed quiet?" Vanessa exclaimed, incredulous.

"I thought it wasn't a big deal," Anne said, her voice small.

"And I sent robots to his house," Lily confessed, looking down. "hmmm Sorry."

"Fine, I have a plan," Anne said, determination replacing her earlier hesitation. "But we need to act fast."

"This is all my fault. My family is in danger because of me," Jalil said, his voice breaking.

"We all made mistakes, but we can fix this," Mike reassured him, placing a comforting hand on his shoulder.

They didn't wait for school to close, instead creating an emergency to use as a cover to escape. Deborah parked haphazardly in front of the foster home, where they returned to gather evidence and trace Nancy's location. As they searched, they found Marc taped to the wall.

"How did you get there?" Lily asked, surprised. As they help him down.

"I'm sorry. I was sent by Hadie to get Nancy, but I realized I made a mistake. I was too scared to tell Nancy, even though she kept insisting on seeing my workplace. Now she's in danger," Marc confessed, his voice filled with remorse.

"We can focus on that later. For now, let's get her back," Anne said, urgency in her voice as they freed Marc and dragged him outside.

"I thought you guys were four," Marc remarked, looking around.

"That's not important right now. Where's your van?" Mike asked.

"They took it," Marc replied.

"Who?" Lily asked, her voice tense.

"Your clones," Marc said, his voice laced with fear.

"How did you know?" Anne asked, surprised.

"I've worked at Hardive for a long time," Marc explained.

"That explains a lot," Jalil said sarcastically.

"Let's just find a cab and go," Marc suggested.

"Or you can all use this car I found," Debby said, appearing with her vehicle to remind them she had a car.

"How did she—" Marc began to ask, but Anne cut him off. "We'll talk about that on the way."

A few minutes later, they arrived at the entrance where they packed the car far from the building and they hid behind the building.

"Can't you just go in?" Debby asked Marc.

"I'm banned," Marc said, pointing to a robot guard with an X mark on its face.

"Look there," Anne said, pointing to a potential entry point.

"We can't get up there. We're not climbers," Lily said, doubt creeping into her voice.

"I have an idea. Debby, do your hands still work?" Jalil asked, then quickly corrected himself. "Sorry, I meant the curse.".

"Yeah, I think so. Why?" Debby asked, curious. "I haven't disintegrated anything for a while" she said.

"Try being negative like the first time we meet" Jalil said she sits silently on the ground and her thoughts begin to spiral she then places her hand on the flower next to the building and they all died

"How did you know that would work" Deborah asked.

“While I was doing my devotion I realized the devil works with negative energy but if you can close it out you can channel the blessing of God through you” Jalil said as she tries thinking happy thoughts, touch the flowers and they bloomed again.

"She is..." Marc began, but Vanessa interrupted, "Yes, she is."

"What do we do now?" Mike asked, looking to the group for guidance.

"We'll go through the vents on the ground, not up there, while Debby distracts them," Jalil suggested.

They made their way to the vents while Debby created a diversion. Inside the building vents, they reached the room where Nancy was held captive, with Hadie inside. The weight of their mission pressed heavily on them, but they knew they had to act to save their friend and set things right.

CHAPTER FOURTEEN

"For Many years I have searched for a descendant of Melaangel but now I found you and have done the test but it keeps on saying she is in your house and you don't want to talk, I would leave you for the Witch and she would drain your power until you finally speak, because this Halloween would be your last" Hadie he declared ominously as he exited.

As the vents creaked open, Nancy turned to see Vanessa, Lily, Mike, Anne, and Marc, "I can't believe I trusted you, Marc," she said, her voice trembling.

"I'm sorry, I was just..." Marc began, but Nancy cut him off. "Just what?"

"If you want to save me, just let Marc not be here," Nancy insisted.

Amidst the tension, Drake and Jalil introduced themselves. "Hi, I'm Drake, and this is Jalil," Drake said.

Jalil rolled his eyes. "Are you serious? They're having a conflict, and you're introducing us?"

"She needs to know us so we won't be strangers," Drake replied, as he goes to relax but accidentally pressed a button. "Oh no" they all said as the alarm blared, and Debby rushed in. "Why would you push the alarm?" she asked, exasperated.

"How did you find us?" Mike inquired.

"When we're safe, I'll explain," Debby promised as they fled the prison room. As they ran, she explained, "Whenever one of my descendants is near or in trouble, I feel like a vibration in my body."

"That's odd and cool at the same time," Drake remarked. Suddenly, Hadie blocked their path. "Not so fast, children. You cannot leave with my properties," he sneered, using a ray gun to capture Nancy and her foster kids. "And as for you, Marc, I told you to leave, but you didn't, so you'll be my second guest after your beloved girlfriend."

As guards restrained Marc, Nancy looked away, not knowing how to feel about Marc.

Jalil stepped forward. "Leave them alone. You are not like this."

Hadie's voice cracked with emotion. "I am like this. Do you think you're the only one tired of being African and suffering all your life? Parents boss you around, and if you don't obey, you're flogged. As the eldest, you're the first housemaid and servant to your siblings. No matter how much you try, you can't impress your parents. They make your efforts worthless," he listed, tears streaming down Jalil's cheeks. "You don't know if you want to be at home because you love your family, but it feels like there's no love. And when you leave Africa, you come to a country where you're made to feel inferior."

"He's winning you over. Fight it. My dad always told me, 'With God, nothing is impossible,'" Debby encouraged. Hadie turned to Debby, taunting, "And as for you, hiding because of your curse, I'm hurting your descendant. Why have I not died?"

"Because I am protecting you, idiot," the Witch interjected.

"You," Debby gasped.

The Witch smirked. "Oh, hello. Nice to meet you finally. I need you to keep doing your work and stop hiding. Did you think changing your name would make you a disciple of Christ? It doesn't, because if it did, I would have been in heaven by now."

Debby stood firm. "Like my father told me, 'We wrestle not against flesh and blood, but against principalities and powers.'"

Finding her resolve, Debby declared, "I should have tried this long ago. I accept Jesus into my life."

A brilliant light shone, and an angel appeared. "These are the words of the Lord: 'Touch not my anointed and do my prophet no harm,'" the angel proclaimed, and the Witch disintegrated in the light. Everything vanished, leaving the group in awe of the miraculous intervention.

CHAPTER FIFTEEN

As Hadie was led away in handcuffs, he shouted, "What happened to my company? You will pay for this!" The police officer replied, "You are under arrest for selling harmful apps."

With Hadie gone, Lily turned to Debby. "Are you free from your curse now?" she asked.

"I think so," Debby replied, gently touching a nearby plant. The leaves bloomed instantly.

"Wow, nice," Jalil commented, sharing a smile with Lily.

“Although I don’t think He was the one or the witch was the one who kept me cursed it was because of myself doubt” Deborah said as she smiled.

“I learnt that from Drake he told me not to always listen to the darkness so it doesn’t consume me” Jalil said

“I’m Glad we found you and I was able to help you like I wanted to” Lily said as they both hug

Nearby, Anne awkwardly hugged Drake. "That was awkward," Anne admitted pulling herself back.

"Yeah," Drake agreed as they laugh nervously, then there was a total silence which they broke as they asked each other out simultaneously, "Can you go out with me?"

"Of course," Drake replied, and Anne kissed his cheek. "See you later then," Anne said, heading over to Debby. "Where is Nancy" Anne asked.

"She's over there," Lily pointed out.

Anne approached Nancy. "Hi, can I sit here?" she asked, and Nancy nodded. "I know I was the one who convinced you, but he did try to correct his wrongs," Anne said as Marc approached, holding flowers.

"Hi, I'm sorry," Marc said softly.

"I need some time alone," Nancy replied, and Anne left them.

Two weeks later, everything had returned to normal. Marc and Nancy were still together after they talked about their issues, while Anne and Drake explored new places in the city. Jalil had become best friends with Lily at least an improvement with his life. They all gathered at Drake's uncle's house for a party, where Jalil was also invited.

During the party, Debby stood on the balcony, staring at the dark sky. Lily noticed and joined her.

"I keep wondering, after all these years, I should be dead, right? But why am I still alive and so young?" Debby pondered.

"At least you're free from the curse. Let's focus on that," Lily suggested.

Jalil, searching for Lily, finally found her. "Hey, Lily, I keep having this weird dream where I see Hadie saying, 'I'm coming for you.'"

"Never mind that. We are safe under God's protection," Lily reassured him.

Meanwhile, Hadie's voice echoed ominously, "I WILL RETURN."

THE END.

EMBRACING YOUR UNIQUE JOURNEY

Life often presents us with challenges, and there are times when things may not go as planned. It's natural to find ourselves wishing we were like someone else—the seemingly perfect sibling, classmate, or colleague. However, it's important to remember that each of us is created and brought into this world for a unique reason. This purpose is intrinsic to who we are, and discovering it is a personal journey that requires introspection and perseverance.

Feeling like you can't do it alone is not a reason to give up. Keep pushing forward, and surround yourself with friends who will stand by your side, offering support and encouragement. True friends help you grow and remind you of your potential when you doubt yourself.

One key lesson I learned while writing this book is that self-perception can be a powerful barrier. You might view yourself as a problem, which can hinder your ability to see yourself as a solution. Deborah, a character in this book, had to learn this lesson, albeit in a way that was perhaps more straightforward than most of us experience. However, the path to self-discovery and fulfillment is rarely easy.

I urge you to persist in your journey. Embrace your individuality, and don't shy away from the challenges that come your way. Remember, every setback is an opportunity to learn and grow. You have the strength and capability to overcome obstacles and achieve your dreams. Believe in yourself, and keep moving forward, because I believe you can do it if you put your mind to it and if it is right with God Luke 1:37.

ACKNOWLEDGEMENT

I would like to begin by expressing my heartfelt gratitude to God, whose grace and guidance have been my constant companions throughout this journey. Your divine presence has been a source of strength, inspiration, and comfort during the challenging moments of writing this book.

To the incredible team at Bluerose, I owe an immense debt of gratitude. Your unwavering support and dedication have been instrumental in bringing this project to fruition. Your regular check-ins and genuine interest in the progress of this book not only kept me accountable but also provided much-needed encouragement when the path seemed daunting.

Bluerose Team

Publication Manager

Special thanks to the publication manager, Rishabh, for your keen eye and insightful feedback. Your expertise has undoubtedly elevated the quality of this work, pushing me to refine my ideas and sharpen my prose. Your guidance throughout the publication process has been invaluable, ensuring that every detail was meticulously addressed.

Project Management

Nick, your organizational skills and timely reminders were crucial in keeping this project on track. Your ability to navigate the complexities of the publishing process while maintaining a supportive atmosphere is truly appreciated.

Personal Support

I am profoundly grateful to my family and friends who have been patient and understanding throughout this process. Your love and encouragement have been my anchor, providing the emotional support needed to see this project through to completion.

To my readers, both future and present, thank you for your interest in this work. It is my sincere hope that you find value, inspiration, and enjoyment in these pages.

Lastly, I want to acknowledge all those who have contributed to my growth as a writer and a person. Your influence, whether direct or indirect, has shaped this book in countless ways.

This journey has been one of collaboration, perseverance, and faith. To everyone who has been a part of it, I offer my deepest and most sincere thanks.

ABOUT THE AUTHOR

Joshua Itiveh, also known as Josio Joti, is a passionate young author with a vision to positively impact lives through his work. He believes in the power of storytelling to entertain, inspire, and foster connection among people. With a deep commitment to his craft, Joshua strives to create narratives that resonate with readers, offering both entertainment and meaningful insights. Although this passion for writing was initially ignited by wanting to follow in the footsteps of someone who at primary school had published a book it's now something he doesn't mind take seriously in fact to help those young writers find their footing and believe they can do it, if they are willing.

His journey as a writer is fuelled by a desire to explore diverse themes and share experiences that reflect the complexities of life. Joshua's writing is characterized by authenticity and a relatable voice, making his stories accessible to a wide audience. He is dedicated to honing his skills and continuously improving as a writer, eager to learn from both successes and challenges.

Joshua's enthusiasm for storytelling is matched by his appreciation for the support he receives from friends, family, and fellow writers. He values their encouragement and feedback, which motivate him to pursue his dreams. As he embarks on this literary journey, Joshua Itiveh remains hopeful about the future, aspiring to leave a lasting impact on the world through his words and creativity.

Don't forget to follow my instagram

Jiswstorypromotionaccount

For more stories which are coming out soon please follow

USE THIS PAGE TO WRITE DOWN
ANYTHING YOU WANT

www.ingramcontent.com/pod-product-compliance
Lightning Source LLC
LaVergne TN
LVHW091112150826
845673LV00002B/786